Topic: Interpersonal Skills   **Subtopic:** Sharing

Note to Parents and Teachers:
Children enter school with a vast understanding of spoken language, but written letters and words are not as familiar. The best way to get children reading is to teach them how to decode words. Begin by teaching that words are made up of phonemes (sounds). Then, teach children the letters that stand for those phonemes. As their decoding abilities get stronger, they will begin to comprehend what they are reading as well. These skills will help them become proficient readers.

Bookends for the Reader!

Here are some reminders before reading the text:
- Look through the pages of the book to get a sense of the story and make a connection to something you already know.
- Focus on letter sounds instead of letter names. Practice sounding out each word letter by letter (sound by sound) and blending the sounds to read words.
- Some words may need to be memorized because they are not decodable.

Words to Know Before You Read

bakes
book
home
like
pie
shade
share
toys

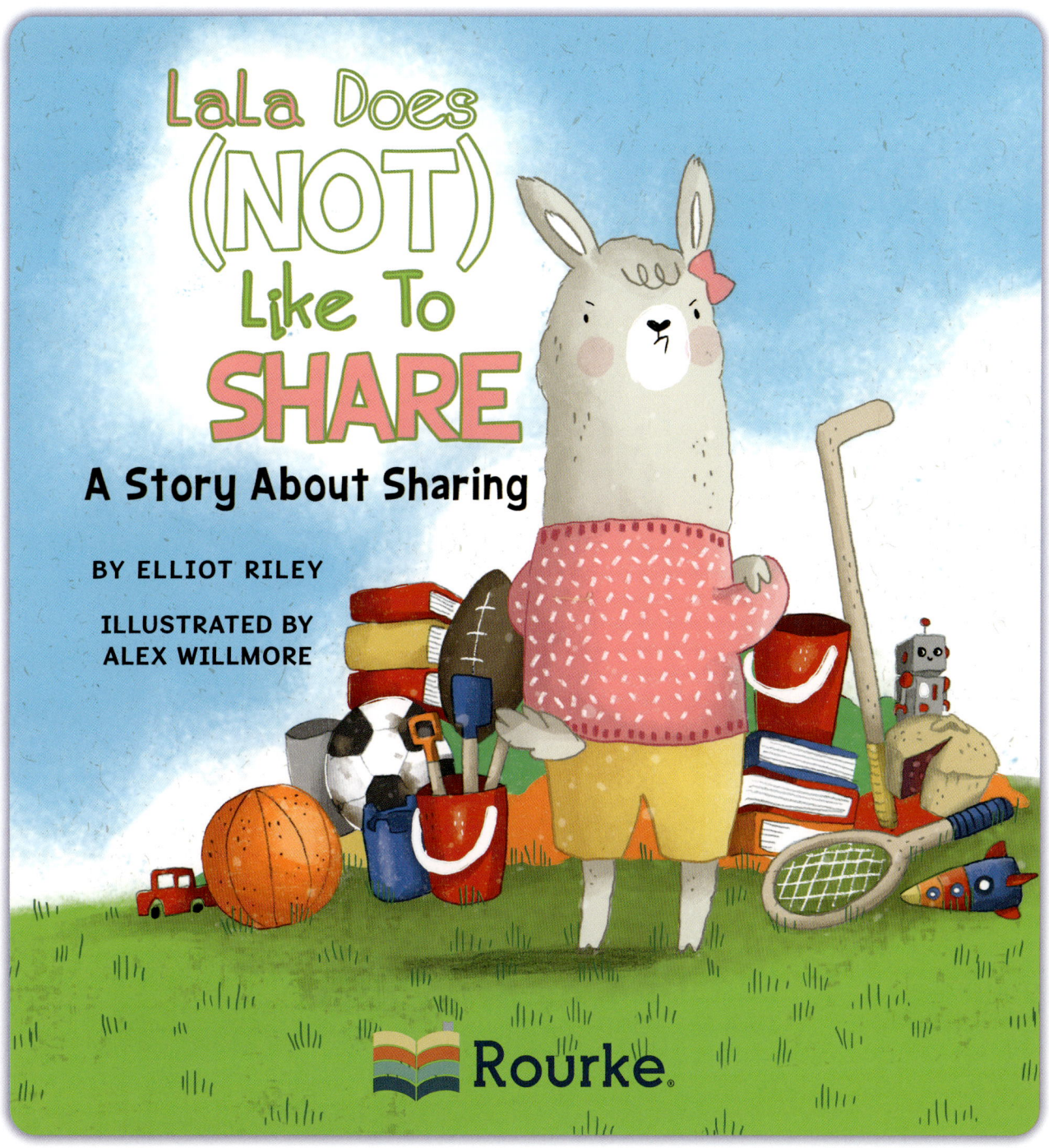

LaLa does not like to share.

"Mine!"

"Mine!"

"Do you want to share my pie?"

"Mine!"

"Do you want to share my toys?"

"Mine!"

"Do you want to share my book?"

"Mine!"

LaLa has lots!

But LaLa is lonely.

At home,

she mixes.

She stirs.

She bakes.

She boxes some books.

She tosses in toys.

"Do you want to share my cake?" she asks.

"Do you want to share my toys?"

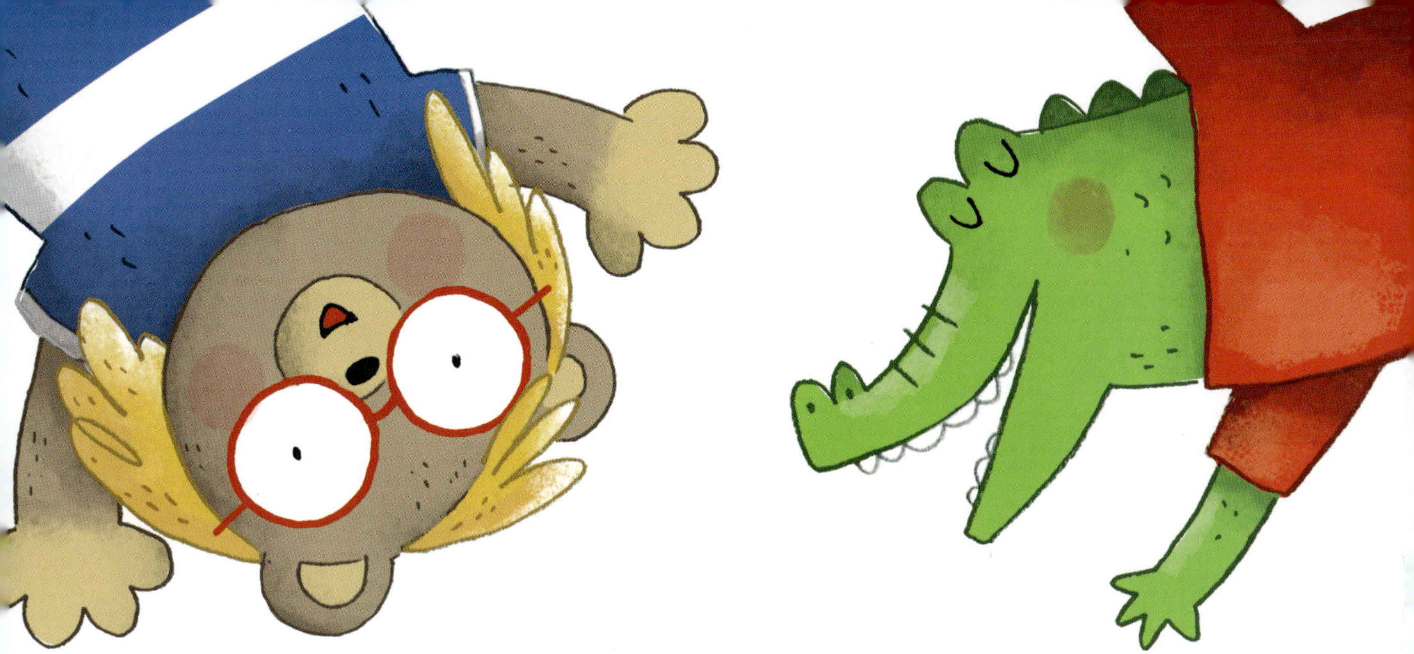

"Yes!" they say.

Bookends for the Reader

I know...

1. What does LaLa do when others offer to share their things with her?

2. What does LaLa go home to make?

3. How does LaLa change at the end of the story?

I think...

1. What do you think made LaLa decide it is better to share?

2. How does sharing help friends get along?

3. Are there some things you should not share? If yes, what are they?

Bookends for the Reader

What happened in this book?
Look at each picture and talk about what happened in the story.

About the Author

Elliot Riley is a writer from Florida who loves to read, explore, and learn about the world. She recently learned that a pumpkin is a fruit! Elliot's favorite moments happen when her children teach her something new.

About the Illustrator

Born in Northampton, England, in 1985, Alex has been drawing characters since the moment he first picked up a pencil.

Library of Congress PCN Data

LaLa Does (Not) Like To Share (A Story About Sharing)/Elliot Riley
(Let's Do It Together)
ISBN 978-1-64156-504-2 (hard cover)
ISBN 978-1-64156-630-8 (soft cover)
ISBN 978-1-64156-740-4 (e-Book)
Library of Congress Control Number: 2018930720

Rourke Educational Media
Printed in Ningbo, Zhejiang, China
07-0202512936

© 2019 Rourke Educational Media

All rights reserved. No part of this book may be reproduced or utilized in any form or by any means, electronic or mechanical including photocopying, recording, or by any information storage and retrieval system without permission in writing from the publisher.

www.rourkebooks.com

Edited by: Keli Sipperley
Layout by: Corey Mills
Cover and interior illustrations by: Alex Willmore